Magic Potions Shop

The Firebird

rd:

The Magic Potions Shop

The Firebird

Abie Longstaff & Lauren Beard

RED FOX

RED FOX

UK I USA I Canada I Ireland I Australia
India I New Zealand I South Africa

Red Fox is part of the Penguin Random House group of companies
whose addresses can be found at global.penguinrandomhouse.com.

www.penguin.co.uk
www.puffin.co.uk
www.ladybird.co.uk

Penguin
Random House
UK

First published 2017

001

Text copyright © Abie Longstaff, 2017
Illustrations copyright © Lauren Beard, 2017

The moral right of the author and illustrator has been asserted

Set in Palatino Regular 16/23pt
Printed in Great Britain by Clays Ltd, St Ives plc

A CIP catalogue record for this book is available from the British Library

ISBN: 978–1–782–95193–3

All correspondence to:
Red Fox
Penguin Random House Children's
80 Strand, London WC2R 0RL

For K & E
– A.L.

For Niall
– L.B.

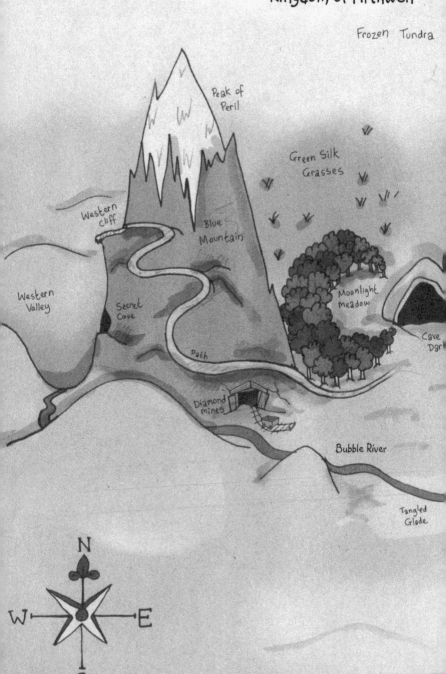

Prince
Oro's
Palace

Lake
Sapphire

The Potions
Tree

Steadysong Forest

Troll Hills

Vale of
years

Eastern shores

Fickle
Ocean

Troll Bridge

Troll Plains

Mouse
Pond.

Vine
Curtain

Parched Desert

Chapter One

It was nearly bedtime at the top of the old tree in Steadysong Forest.

"Another cup of tea, Grandpa?" Tibben poked his head into Grandpa's bedroom. The room was almost dark; the only light came from a little lamp on the side table.

"No thank you, Tibben." Grandpa yawned. "I think I'll just go to sleep now."

"OK." Tibben gently closed the

door. He frowned.
Grandpa was tired all
the time nowadays!
He was nearly one
hundred years
old and soon
he would
retire to the Vale
of Years. Tibben chewed his lip.

Grandpa was the Potions Master
– it was his job to make potions
and creams and ointments to help
the creatures of Arthwen. In his
long career, Grandpa had been
all over the kingdom, helping
Thunder Goblins in the Diamond
Mines, Fluff Griffins on the Peak
of Peril and Sea Gnomes under the

Fickle Ocean. His cloak shone with hundreds of **Glints**, the magical sign of potions skill. But soon, when he turned a hundred, his cloak would stop sparkling. All the **Glints** that covered the fabric would disappear and Grandpa would have to stop being the Potions Master.

Then the Kingdom of Arthwen would need a new one. Tibben fingered the fabric of his own cloak. He had four **Glints** now – *Crystal*, *Opal*, *Pearl* and **Ruby**. He needed **Diamond** level; then he would be allowed to take the Master's Challenge to become a Potions Master just like Grandpa.

His training was nearly complete, and yet . . . yet . . . Tibben still didn't always get everything right.

Every day customers came to the Potions Shop. Every day they rang the bluebell and pushed open the door in the tree. Every day Tibben tried to make potions to help them, but sometimes it all went wrong.

This morning, without Grandpa to help, Tibben had accidentally made **Tail Powder** instead of **Trail Powder** for a Hunting Imp. He shook his head, remembering how cross the imp had

4

been to end up with a metre-long green tail. Grandpa had had to get out of bed and come all the way downstairs to the Potions Shop to remove the tail with *Elixir of Nature* and make a proper batch of **Trail Powder**.

"You have to be more careful, Tibben," he had said.

"I'm sorry, Grandpa. I guess I just misheard him."

"And you know you're supposed to test your potions before you give them out."

"I know, I know," said Tibben miserably. "I'm sorry."

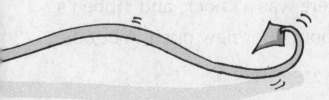

Now, Tibben opened the door to his little room and sat down on his bed. Ever since Grandpa had been taken ill the world had felt funny – the air was heavy and misty and it seemed like nothing was going right. Tibben was so desperate to fix things! He had hardly slept from worrying about it.

He had to get his next **Glint** soon. He just had to! He couldn't bear the idea of not being ready when Grandpa retired. What would happen to Arthwen if there was no Potions Master? Tibben didn't like to think about it.

There was a knock, and Tibben's bedroom door flew open. A bundle

of white fluff came bouncing in and jumped on his bed.

"Wizz!" Tibben cried. It was always lovely to see Wizz – she could make him feel better with just a hug. "How was your Gathering?" She had been out all day finding ingredients to refill the jars on the shelves of the Potions Shop.

"Good wooz!" Wizz opened her
Gathering Diary and showed
Tibben drawings of all the plants
she had collected.

"Oo, **Steady Leaf**," said Tibben
as she pointed to a flat green shape
she had pressed between the pages.
"That's really useful for **Singsong
Potion** – the birds will need that

now spring is here." He turned a page. "And you found *Cloud Lotus* for **Dreaming Potion**!"

"Yes, yes!" Wizz cried proudly.

"I could use a nice dream tonight." Tibben frowned. "I'd love to get a good night's sleep."

Wizz put her soft paws around his neck. "No worry wooz," she said. "Glint soon come."

"Do you think so?"

"Yes, Wizz sure."

Tibben smiled and hugged her. Already he felt better. Wizz was right – he'd get his next Glint soon; he just had to keep trying.

He looked across the room to his little window. Outside, night was falling and the moon shone down over Steadysong Forest. Tibben could hear the Bearded Frogs croaking and the Wolf Crickets chirping. There was a sudden rumble as a Twilight Unicorn

galloped past on his way home to Moonlight Meadow. Tibben slowly began to feel happy and warm. He smiled. "Thanks, Wizz," he said.

Chapter Two

In the morning the sun woke
Tibben. He yawned and stretched
and rubbed his eyes. He could hear
Wizz bouncing around in her room,
just along the corridor. He stood up
and pulled on his cloak, ready to
start the day.

Down the wooden stairs he
climbed, twisting round and round
inside the tree, until he came to
the Potions Shop at the bottom.

The shop was quiet and still before all the customers came in. Tibben looked up at the rows and rows of shelves holding thousands of jars and bottles and pots, all full of ingredients and potions to treat every kind of problem. From here he could see **Long Beard Gel** (especially useful for Dwarfs and Bearded Frogs), **Hover Potion**

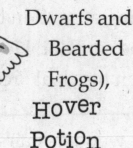

and **Iron Cream**, used to repair broken shells and horns.

Grandpa had asked Tibben to practise **Blooming Brew**, a kind of health potion, today. Yesterday, for some reason, several customers from the south had come to complain that their vegetables weren't growing well. Tibben had had to give out so much **Blooming Brew** that the jar was nearly empty!

"Morning, morning!" Wizz sang as she jumped down the last three steps.

"Good morning, Wizz." Tibben smiled as he lifted up a heavy red leather book. This was *The Book of Potions*. He turned the pages until he found:

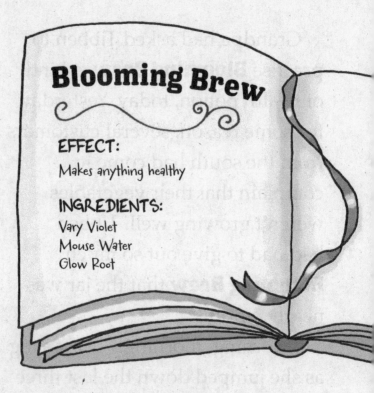

Blooming Brew

EFFECT:
Makes anything healthy

INGREDIENTS:
Vary Violet
Mouse Water
Glow Root

"I hope I get this right . . ." He read through the list of ingredients. *Vary Violet* grew in the Frozen Tundra. Wizz had found some when they went to help Karhu, the Blizzard Bear. *Mouse Water* came

from a pond near Vine Curtain.
Wizz had collected it when they
went to help the River Horse. In
the Potions Shop, both ingredients
were kept underground in the
cellar, where it was cool and dark.

"Wizz," said Tibben. "Do you
mind getting the *Vary Violet* and
the *Mouse Water* for me?" Wizz
was so quick. She hung from the
tree-root steps by her tail and could
be down and back from the cellar
much faster
than Tibben.
"Thank you!"
he called
as she opened
the hatch.

Tibben turned back to the counter, and as his cloak swished, he caught sight of his **Glints** sparkling at him. He smiled. He couldn't wait to reach **Diamond** level! What would a **Diamond Glint** look like? It was bound to be really sparkly and shiny! Tibben was distracted as he searched the shelves for **Glow Root** – he was so distracted that he didn't notice his fingers had closed around a jar of *Low Root*. He took an extra-large pinch and ground it up in his **Mage Nut** bowl.

Wizz popped up from the cellar

with the other ingredients.

"Thanks, Wizz," said Tibben.
He chopped the *Vary Violet* and
poured the *Mouse Water* until
the mixture turned into a brightly
coloured liquid. Now it was time
to test it!

Tibben took a big sip of the
strange liquid. All of a sudden he
felt dizzy. The world seemed to be
moving in a weird way.

"Ooooh!"
he cried,
and the
next thing
he knew, he
had shrunk
right down to

the size of a Mud Bug. Wizz
towered over him, a huge
grin on her enormous face.

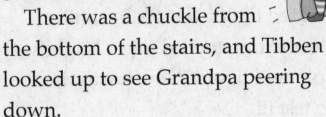

There was a chuckle from
the bottom of the stairs, and Tibben
looked up to see Grandpa peering
down.

"Ah, Tibben, I think you might
have used Low Root instead
of **Glow Root**. You've made a
wonderful **Shrinking** Potion there."

Tibben gazed around. The shop
looked massive. The jars and pots
were gigantic, and it was miles from
the floor to the wooden counter.
He waggled his little arms. "Wizz,
can you lift me up!" he cried in a
squeaky voice.

Wizz scooped him up on her paw and put him on the counter.

Tibben climbed onto his **Mage Nut** spoon and sat on the wide handle. "Oops," he said.

Grandpa and Wizz were chortling and holding their tummies. Tibben looked at his teeny tiny fingers and started to giggle.

Chapter Three

While Grandpa made a big pot of **Blooming Brew**, Tibben sat on the counter until the Shrinking Potion had worn off.

"Thanks, Grandpa," he said, once he had returned to his normal size. "Sorry . . . again."

"It's OK, Tibben," said Grandpa, "but you need to slow down and read everything properly."

Tibben nodded. He felt miserable.

Ding-dong! went the bluebell of the Potions Shop.

"Come on," said Grandpa, ruffling Tibben's hair. "Why don't you see who needs our help now?"

Wham!

The door of the shop flew open, and a large Quarry Troll poked his

enormous head in through the doorway.

"Good morning!" he boomed.

"Morning," called Tibben as he hurried over. There was no way the troll would fit into the shop so Tibben had to meet him outside. He stepped out and looked up . . . and up . . . and up. The Quarry Troll was massive – as tall as the Potions Tree!

"How can I help?" asked Tibben.

The troll opened his knobbly grey hand and Tibben climbed on. The troll lifted him up into the air and onto his shoulder.

"My name's Cragg," he said. "I'm looking for some kind of

potion for my garden."

Another customer with a problem garden! "What's wrong?" Tibben asked.

"It's strange," said Cragg. "My vegetables are all dying. I looked at the soil and it's covered in sand."

"Sand?" Tibben frowned. "That is strange."

Quarry Trolls came from the Troll
Plains. There wasn't any sand
there – unless . . . unless . . . "The
Troll Plains – they're near the
Parched Desert, aren't they?"
he asked.

"Yes," said Cragg, "and it's been
so windy lately, the sand is blowing
in and covering our land."

"Hmm," said Tibben. "It
shouldn't be so windy in the desert."

"It's an odd kind of wind," said
the troll. "It only comes every now
and then. But each gust from the
desert blows a big pile of sand
into the plains. It's ruining our
vegetables and the little trolls hate
it – it makes their eyes sting."

Tibben shivered. Something wasn't right. "Put me down and I'll get you some **Blooming Brew**," he said.

He rushed into the shop and came back out, struggling with the huge pot Grandpa had made.

"Thank you," said Cragg, and he waved goodbye.

"Grandpa, Grandpa!" cried Tibben, bursting back through the door. "I think there's a problem in the desert!"

Grandpa sat down in the waiting chair and pulled a round golden object out of his pocket – this was the *Master's Dial*. It measured Harmony and Blight. A little arrow on its face moved between H, for when everything was right with the kingdom, and B, for when something was wrong.

"Hmm," said the old pixie, frowning.

Tibben peered over his shoulder and gasped. The arrow was nearly at B! "Oh no!" he said in a panic. "I've never seen so much Blight!"

"Calm down, my boy," said Grandpa. "I've been feeling the signs of Blight for a little while now."

"Me too," Tibben said. There was

a feeling of emptiness and sadness in the air. It was as if Arthwen knew there would soon be no Potions Master.

"I have to get that **Glint** and take the Master's Challenge," Tibben said.

"Yes – in time. But first you need to find out what's causing the gusts of wind," Grandpa told him.

"Wizz and I will go straight away," said Tibben.

Grandpa nodded. "And I'll make some potions for the journey."

Tibben rushed upstairs to get his backpack. "Wizz," he called.

"Weez?"

"We're off to the Parched Desert!"

"Woozoo!" cried Wizz. She loved going to new places. Everywhere they went she found special plants and seeds for Grandpa's potions.

Tibben smiled – it would be good to get out into the fresh air. And it would be fun to see a new part of Arthwen! Tibben had never been to the desert before. He knew from Grandpa that it was a hot and dry place, where Oven Scorpions scuttled across rocks, and Oil Ants made homes underground. "Come on, Wizz! Let's go!"

Wizz grabbed her Gathering Diary, and together they ran down the stairs to say goodbye to Grandpa.

"Good luck," he said, handing them a jar of Cooling Potion. "You'll need this for the heat," he explained.

Wizz helped Tibben pack the potion away. Then she reached for the potions he had made earlier: the Trail Powder and the Shrinking Potion.

"What are you doing, Wizz?" Tibben asked as she sprinkled some **Trail Powder** into a leaf and rolled it up.

"Take all potions, wooz," she explained.

"Good idea." Grandpa nodded. "You never know what you might need."

Tibben shrugged and squeezed everything into his backpack, along with *The Book of Potions*. Then he fastened a bottle of water to his belt

and tied his **Mage Nut** bowl to the outside of his bag.

"Bye, Grandpa!"

"Bye wooz!"

"Goodbye! Don't forget to look out for ingredients," Grandpa called. "We especially need **Red-Hot Orchid** for *Exploding Powder*."

Wizz gave him a thumbs-up
while Tibben checked the map.
"South," he said, and set off.

Chapter Four

Tibben and Wizz walked quickly through Steadysong Forest. In the distance they could just make out the figure of Cragg, who was going home to his family. Tibben put away the map – from here on they could follow the path the troll had made as he crashed through the trees.

Wizz paused to sniff the air now and then, her fur standing up when she sensed something useful. She

stopped by a bright
red flower and
pulled on a pair
of gloves to strip
some leaves off
its stem.

"**Red-Hot Orchid**!"
said Tibben. "Nice work, Wizz."

She sat down for a moment, drew
a picture of the orchid and made a
note of where she had found it.

Soon they came to the southern
edge of Steadysong Forest. Now
they had to cross the Troll Plains
to reach the Parched Desert. They
stepped out of the shelter of the
trees, and

Whoosh!

There was a sudden gust of hot wind.

Tibben shut his eyes as tiny grains of sand hit his face, stinging his cheeks. "Ow!" he cried.

Then, just as suddenly, the wind was gone. Tibben looked down. The soil underfoot was speckled with fine yellow dots of sand. "Something about that wind feels very strange," he said.

Wizz nodded. She turned and picked a large Shelter Leaf to protect her face in case the wind came again.

"That's clever, Wizz," said Tibben, and she picked one for him too.

As they walked south into the
Troll Plains, they could see the
enormous Troll Bridge to the east.
It looked truly magnificent; it
was carved out of stone from the
Troll Hills. Troll Bridge connected
Steadysong Forest with the Eastern
Shores; in the distance, past the

bridge, Tibben could see the
sparkling Fickle Ocean. He felt a
bubble of love for Arthwen build up
inside him – it was so beautiful!

Wizz sniffed and dashed off to
pick some bright green Grass
Berries, used for making
Budding Potion.

"Well done, Wizz," said Tibben. "Grandpa always needs **Budding Potion** for gardening." He carefully packed the green Grass Berries in his backpack.

"Oh, hello!" he called to a Racing Snail zooming towards him. The snail waggled a hello with his antennae.

All of a sudden there was another blast of hot wind, as if someone had just opened an oven door. The snail curled up into his shell. Tibben and Wizz held their Shelter Leaf umbrellas over their faces to block the wind.

"I wish I had a shell like that to crawl into," Tibben grumbled as small grains of sand hit his legs.

When the gust stopped, the Racing Snail peeped out and shook his head sadly, before speeding off across Troll Bridge.

"I'm going to try and fix it!" called Tibben as the snail raced on his way. "Oh, I hope I can, Wizz . . . Wizz?"

She was standing stock still, her nose pointing upwards and her whiskers sticking out.

"What is it?" asked Tibben.

"Can you sense something?"

Wizz moved a little way ahead and bent down. When she stood up, she had a pile of strange feathers in her paw. The feathers were bright orange, and shimmered in the heat.

"Ow!" she cried, and dropped them quickly again. "Hot hot!"

Tibben bent down too. He held his hand over the feathers. There was a strong heat coming off them.

"Strange," he said. There was something funny about those feathers. Surely they shouldn't be so hot.

Tibben looked up and saw that a trail of feathers led south, towards the Parched Desert. He shivered.

"Come on, Wizz," he said. "Let's follow those feathers."

Chapter Five

"Wizz! We're here!" Tibben pointed to the first sand dune of the Parched Desert and felt a leap of excitement. He took Wizz's paw, and together the friends rushed forward.

Climbing the dune was hard work. With every step they took they sank a little. Just as they reached the top there was another gust of hot wind, and Tibben lifted his Shelter Leaf to stop the sand hitting his face.

Out of the corner of his eye he saw something in the distance that looked like a yellow cloud. It was low to the ground and it seemed to be moving towards them, getting bigger and bigger.

"Weez?" Wizz raised her eyebrows.

"I don't know what it is," said Tibben, "but I don't like it."

The yellow cloud came closer

and closer, and he started to panic.

"I think it's a sand storm!" he cried. "Oh, Wizz! It's going to hit us!" His heart was thumping.

They held up their Shelter Leaves, but the wind lifted the leaves high in the air and blew them away. Frantically Tibben looked around for something else to hide behind.

The storm was coming closer!

The hot wind blew sand into their faces. Suddenly Tibben spotted an old snail shell. *That shell would be perfect to hide in*, he thought; *if only we were the size of a snail . . .*

Of course!

"Wizz!" he shouted over the wind. "Where's the Shrinking Potion?" He tipped out his bag, and Wizz spotted the potion at once.

"Quick!" cried Tibben. "The sand storm is nearly here!"

Wizz took a sip and shrank down right away. Tibben followed her down, down, down – until they were so tiny they could crawl into the empty shell.

It was dark inside, and Tibben

and Wizz
cuddled up
together
as they
heard the
storm raging
outside. Tibben
closed his eyes. The
Shrinking Potion would only last ten
minutes. *I really hope the storm is over
soon*, he said to himself, shivering.
It seemed the closer they got to the
centre of the desert, the stronger
the bursts of wind were becoming.
What would they find at the centre?
He nibbled his lip and buried his
head in Wizz's fur. "I'm so glad
you're here," he told her.

Tibben and Wizz waited and
waited until the wind died down.

"I think the storm's gone," said
Tibben at last.

"Quiet wooz," said Wizz, and
Tibben nodded. In fact, it was now
so quiet that all he could hear was
a scratch-scratching sound. *Hang
on . . .* he thought. *What is making
that noise?*

"Wizz," he whispered, "there's
something in here with us!"

"Hello wooz?" called Wizz.

There was an answering
drumming on the base of the shell.
Tibben peered into the darkness and
made out the shape of a creature.

"It's OK," he said. "I'm the

Potions Apprentice
and I'm here to help.
Let's all get out into
the light."

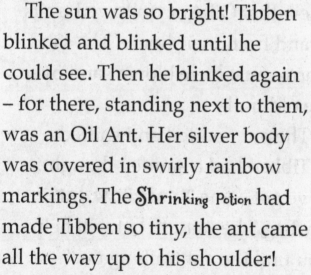

One by one they
crawled out of the old
snail shell.

The sun was so bright! Tibben
blinked and blinked until he
could see. Then he blinked again
– for there, standing next to them,
was an Oil Ant. Her silver body
was covered in swirly rainbow
markings. The Shrinking Potion had
made Tibben so tiny, the ant came
all the way up to his shoulder!

"Hello," he said, but the ant
didn't hear him. She was too busy

turning round and round in circles, as if she was looking for something.

Then she sat down, confused.

"What's wrong?" asked Tibben. "Have you lost your way?" He knew that Oil Ants followed trails to and from their home. The sand storm must have blown sand over the old trails.

The ant nodded and sniffed.

Tibben had a sudden thought. "I've got some **Trail Powder** in my bag," he said. "That will help you find the ant trails again."

The Oil Ant smiled.

"But we've got to get it out of the

bag somehow." Tibben gazed up at his backpack. He was so tiny that it looked gigantic!

He and Wizz crawled into the opening. The huge jars and bottles clinked together as they walked carefully between them.

At the bottom of the bag they found a long, rolled-up leaf. It looked like a giant carpet.

"You take one end and I'll take the other," said Tibben, and he hoisted his end onto his shoulder. Wizz picked up the other end, and together, huffing and puffing, they carried the leaf carpet out of the bag and set it down on the sand.

Tibben crawled into the little opening at one end of the leaf and came back with a large handful of **Trail Powder**.

"Try this," he said, and the ant stuck out her tongue for the powder.

Next she felt along the sand with her antennae. Then she looked up and grinned, and waved her leg.

Tibben smiled. "Hooray – you found the trail!" he cheered.

In thanks, the Oil Ant gave them some of her Antenna Hairs. They looked like large grey sticks in Tibben's hand.

"Thank wooz," said Wizz.

"*Oooh oooh!*" cried Tibben. He was beginning to grow! He felt like he was being stretched out. Up and up he grew until he was back to normal. He looked down at his hand; now the sticks were teeny tiny hairs. He saw that the little Oil Ant was scurrying away to find her colony.

"Goodbye!" he called.

Tibben and Wizz walked on, still following the trail of feathers. The desert was empty. As far as the eye could see there was just sand; yellow sand going for miles and miles. There was no sign of any animal. No Oven Scorpions, no Fever Foxes and no Sizzle Spiders.

"This is very strange," said Tibben.

Wizz stopped and sniffed the air again. She knelt down and dug down into the powdery sand.

"What are you looking for?" asked Tibben.

Suddenly Wizz cried out in triumph: she was holding up a small pawful of berries that were round and see-through.

Tibben couldn't find any mention of them in *The Book of Potions*. "I don't know what you've found there, Wizz, but it looks like it's something special."

Wizz smiled and hugged the strange berries.

Chapter Six

Through the hot desert they
trudged; on and on, keeping their
eyes on the feather trail. They
were both so tired – they had been
walking for hours! Tibben felt like
his mind was playing tricks on him.
He kept seeing shade and water
ahead, only to find that it was just
a mirage, a trick of the light, and
there was nothing there; only more
sand stretching before them. The

air was thick and heavy with mist, and Tibben was beginning to think they'd never find the source of the Blight.

He stopped and sighed and tried to shake the bad feeling away.

Wizz touched his hand with her paw and Tibben looked down at her.

"No worry, wooz," she said, and he smiled.

All at once he remembered: Grandpa had packed them some *Cooling Potion*!

"Here . . ." he said, opening the bottle. "Have a sip, Wizz."

Wizz took it and grinned. She handed the bottle back to Tibben,

and he lifted it to his lips. The
potion tasted wonderful! It slipped
down the back of his throat like icy
water, and he felt like he had just
stepped into a nice cold shower.

"Ah, that's so much better!" he
said.

"Fresh fresh!" said Wizz.

When Tibben looked up again,
he saw a tall figure in the distance.
"Is that another mirage, Wizz?
What do you think?"

Wizz screwed up her nose and
twitched her whiskers. "Elf wooz,"
she said.

"An elf? Are you sure?" asked
Tibben. Elves usually lived on
Blue Mountain.

Wizz nodded. "Elf," she said again.

Tibben headed towards the shape. As he got closer, he realized that Wizz was right! It was an elf, but not like any elf Tibben had ever seen before. Most elves were pale and elegant, with soft skin that shone like moonlight. This one was yellow. His skin was tough and leathery, his body round and stocky. He was standing staring into the distance.

"Hello!" called Tibben in greeting.

The elf turned in surprise. "The Potions Master!" he said, his eyes fixed on Tibben's cloak. "My goodness!"

"I'm Tibben, the Potions

Apprentice," said Tibben, showing his **Glints**. "This is Wizz. We've come to find out what's wrong."

"I'm Sunako, the Sand Elf," the elf answered. "I'm so pleased you came. We need your help."

"Funny wind weez," said Wizz.

"Yes. I don't know what that wind is," said Sunako. "It blows such hot air and brings terrible sand storms."

Tibben nodded.

"Everything feels very odd," the elf went on. "I haven't seen anyone for days. The wind is forcing us all to hide away and it's hard to work. It's my job to find Water Crystals so everyone can drink the fresh water inside, but the sand storms keep covering everything up."

"I'm going to find out what's causing the wind," said Tibben. "I promise I'll help in any way I can."

"Wizz help too," said Wizz.

"Wizz find." She closed her eyes and slowly turned around in a circle, sniffing the air as she moved.

Sunako's eyes widened as he watched her. "What is she doing?" he asked.

"She's a Gatherer," Tibben said proudly. "She's amazing. She can find anything!"

Wizz stopped. She pointed down at the ground, and Sunako began to dig with his spade.

It wasn't long before he pulled
out a handful of shiny blue objects.

"Water Crystals!" he cried,
breaking one open and drinking
the clean fresh water inside. "That's
wonderful! Thank you, Wizz."

The elf handed Wizz a crystal.
"Please take one."

Wizz grinned and packed it away in her bag.

They waved goodbye to the elf.

"Good luck!" Sunako called as they headed off.

Chapter Seven

The trail of feathers was growing
thicker and hotter. Tibben still
had no idea where they had come
from, or what could be causing the
strange winds.

Wizz lifted her nose. "Burning
weez," she said.

Tibben sniffed. He couldn't smell
anything, but Wizz had a much
better sense of smell than he had.
Then, after a while, Tibben started

to smell it too. It was a smell of smoke and bonfires. Just ahead, a shape caught his eye. He couldn't work out what it was.

"Bird wooz," said Wizz.

As they drew closer, Tibben realized that she was right. It was a bird; a very strange bird. It was huge! Its feathers were bright orange and red and yellow, and at the very edges flames were sparking.

"Wizz," breathed Tibben, "I think that's Seraphin the Firebird!"

Grandpa had told Tibben

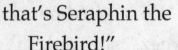

all about the Firebird. Along with the River Horse and Darnöf the Dragon, she was one of the special creatures of Arthwen. The River Horse kept the waters flowing; Darnöf looked after the skies; and Seraphin brought warmth, energy and life to the kingdom.

Seraphin lived for a hundred years; then, on her final day, she built a special nest and filled it with magic fire. The flames turned her back into an egg and, in time, Seraphin hatched out of the egg as a new Firebird, starting her life all over again. Her magic powers meant she could live for ever, helping Arthwen to stay warm and happy, and bringing Harmony to the kingdom. Tibben knew how important she was; he felt very honoured to meet her.

But as the pixie gazed at the mighty bird, he saw that she looked tired and pale. Her wings were ragged and there were feathers missing. Her flames burned brightly, but her eyes were full of tears.

"Poor Seraphin," said Tibben.

"Something is wrong."

"Sad weez." Wizz nodded.

The Firebird suddenly began to flap her wings. A blast of fiery heat hit Tibben and Wizz, and all at once they were knocked to the ground in a cloud of feathers.

"That's what's causing the gusts of hot wind," whispered Tibben to Wizz as he helped her up. "She must be in trouble."

Tibben approached the Firebird nervously. He bowed low, watching out for the bird's sharp pink talons.

"I am Tibben, the Potions Apprentice," he said. His **Glints** shone in the burning light. "Please let me help."

"Tibben," croaked Seraphin. "Thank you for coming. But I fear you are too late." She closed her eyes for a moment to rest.

"What's wrong?" he asked.

"I'm burning up," said the Firebird sadly. "I should have built

my nest, but I hurt my tail and
I couldn't fly to collect the right
plant."

Tibben's eyes widened as he
understood the problem: if Seraphin

couldn't make a nest, she wouldn't be able to turn into an egg. She would just get hotter and hotter – until she disappeared. Then there would be no more Firebird . . . and . . . and Arthwen would be out of balance. Without the energy and fire of the Firebird, everyone would be tired and cold. Tibben shivered. No wonder Blight was getting stronger!

"This is terrible!" he cried.

"I have tried my best to stay cool," said Seraphin. "I've been flapping my wings to fan myself, but it's no use. I keep getting hotter and hotter."

"We'll help you," said Tibben.

"You can't." Seraphin shook her head sadly. "I make my nest out of Fire Lily, but it is so rare, only a Firebird can find it. But now I'm too tired to sense it."

"Wizz is a Gatherer!" Tibben told her. "Wizz! Wizz! Can you find it?"

Wizz closed her eyes for a long time. Then she shook her head sadly.

Tibben's heart started pounding. The Blight was growing more powerful. "Please, Wizz," he said in a small voice. "The air is so heavy and thick."

Wizz's eyes filled with tears. She shook her head. "Sorry wooz," she said. "Wizz not find."

Tibben began to shake. He could feel a hopelessness coming over him like a cloud. If only Grandpa were here! He would know what to do. He looked at Wizz in panic.

Wizz climbed up and flung her arms around his neck. "Sorry!" she cried again.

"It's not your fault, Wizz," said Tibben. "If only I could help you sense it . . . Wait . . ." he said. "Maybe I can. Maybe there's something in here . . ." He picked up *The Book of Potions*.

Chapter Eight

Frantically, Tibben turned the pages of *The Book of Potions*. He looked and looked until he found a recipe that might help. In his panic, he read the recipe as quickly as he could. It said:

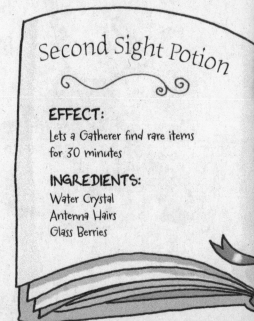

Second Sight Potion

EFFECT:
Lets a Gatherer find rare items for 30 minutes

INGREDIENTS:
Water Crystal
Antenna Hairs
Glass Berries

"We got a Water Crystal from Sunako," said Tibben.

"Hair wooz," said Wizz.

"Yes! We have the Antenna Hairs from the Oil Ant. And we have the Grass Berries you picked on the Troll Plains!" He pulled out the ingredients as fast as he could.

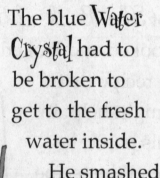

The blue Water Crystal had to be broken to get to the fresh water inside. He smashed it and poured the liquid into his

Mage Nut bowl. He threw in the
Antenna Hairs and mixed them in
with his spoon at top speed. His
heart was pounding in his chest and
his hands were fumbling with the
spoon.

"Now the Grass Berries,"
he said, shoving his hand into
the bottom of his bag. "Although
Grass Berries are a strange
ingredient for this potion . . ." He
frowned. His hands were shaking as
he rummaged for the green berries
in his backpack.

Wizz put her paw on his hand.
He looked at her and stopped for a
moment. Then he remembered what
Grandpa had said: *Slow down and*

read everything properly.

Tibben closed his eyes and breathed in and out slowly. Then he opened his eyes and read the recipe one more time. It needed Water Crystal and Antenna Hairs and . . .

"Oh!" cried Tibben. It wasn't Grass Berries! It was *Glass Berries!*

"What are *Glass Berries?*" he said.

"Wizz find," said Wizz. She pulled the see-through berries she had picked earlier out of her bag.

"Are those *Glass Berries,* Wizz?" Tibben asked her. She nodded. Tibben looked at the berries. They were completely clear.

He smiled. *Glass Berries* made much more sense in this potion than **Grass Berries**!

Tibben grinned. "Let's make *Second Sight Potion!*" he said.

He squeezed the *Glass*

Berries until their juice made the mixture clear like water.

"That's it, I think," he said.

"Wait," said the Firebird. "You'll need to be higher to see the Fire Lily." She struggled to lift herself up. "If only I hadn't hurt my tail I could fly you."

Tibben's face broke into a wide grin. He rummaged in his bag and pulled out the Tail Powder.

"Let's try this!" he said. He rubbed the powder onto the bird's broken tail, and in no time at all new feathers had grown, thick and fiery.

Seraphin smiled. There was a bright gleam in her eyes. "Let's fly!" she said.

The Firebird

Chapter Nine

Tibben stepped back as the mighty
Firebird rose a little way into the air.
She was so beautiful! She glowed
yellow and orange and the tips of her
enormous wings melted into flames.

Gently she picked Tibben and
Wizz up in her long talons. Tibben
gulped as the claws closed around
him. Slowly he felt himself being
lifted up, up, up until he was
floating above the sand.

"Drink the potion now, little Wizz," said Seraphin weakly. "I'm so tired I can't fly for long."

Wizz lifted the **Mage Nut** bowl and took a sip. She closed her eyes.

Tibben watched the land below, keeping his eyes peeled for any sign of plants. From up high, he was looking down onto the sand

dunes. The land was hot and dry.
Any greenery on the desert shrubs
had been blown away to leave spiky
brown branches. Tibben caught sight
of a Fever Fox desperately looking
for shade.

Suddenly Wizz grabbed his hand
with her paw. "Water wooz," she
said.

Tibben couldn't see any sign of water, but the Firebird flew on to where Wizz had pointed.

As they flew over another sand dune, Tibben gasped – down below them was water! Wizz had managed to sense a hidden oasis.

"Hooray! Let us go here!" he cried, and the Firebird opened her talons.

Down, down, down they fell, and *Splash!*

into the cool clear water.

Tibben came up for air and
scrambled to the bank, but Wizz
dived to the bottom in search of
the Fire Lily.

Tibben sat on the bank and
the Firebird landed next to him.
Together they watched for Wizz.
They waited . . . and waited . . .

Suddenly Wizz shot to the surface
with an armful of red flowers! "Lily
wooz," she said, swimming to the
bank.

Tibben beamed. "You found it!"
He helped his friend out of the
water.

"Thank you," said the Firebird. She took the pile of Fire Lily in her beak and pushed it into place under her feathers. Then she looked at them with her big yellow eyes. She bowed and the two friends bowed back.

"I will come and see you when I am reborn," said Seraphin softly. "It will be an honour to visit such a wonderful team. Now stand back, please."

Tibben and Wizz did as the Firebird asked, and the flames around her began to rise higher and higher and grow hotter and hotter. Soon she was covered in fire!

Tibben and Wizz watched in

amazement as, all at once, the
flames disappeared in a cloud of
smoke. The friends stepped forward
to see what remained. And there
in the embers, exactly where the

Firebird had stood, was a bright red egg.

"We did it," said Tibben, hugging Wizz. He breathed in. The air felt clear now; fresh and light.

"Woozoo!" Wizz cheered. She climbed up and threw her fluffy paws around his neck.

As Tibben swung her round and round, he noticed something shining on his cloak: a **Glint**! He had earned a **Diamond Glint**!

"Wow!" he said, and Wizz stood back to admire it. The **Glint** was even more sparkly than Tibben had imagined. It shone bright, reflecting the yellows of the desert.

He looked at Wizz. "Wizz!" he

said in wonder. "It's so beautiful!"

Wizz grinned at him. "Grandpa wooz," she said.

"Yes! Let's show Grandpa," said Tibben, and he took her paw as they walked home.

Chapter Ten

The air was much calmer now that
the blasts of hot wind had stopped.
Tibben smiled. He could feel that
Harmony was flowing back into
the land. The desert shrubs and
bushes unfurled their leaves, the
sound of Blaze Swallows filled the
sky and everything was right in the
kingdom.

Wizz was bouncing along beside
him, happily sniffing the air for

plants. She managed to pick **Flame Thorn** and *Spark Leaf* to make **Firework Liquid** and **Pepper Nettle** for **Sharpening Ointment**. She drew each plant carefully in her **Gathering Diary** and Tibben looked them up in *The Book of Potions*.

As the friends passed through the Parched Desert, creatures came out of their holes and burrows to wave in thanks. Oven Scorpions shook their poisonous tails, Fever Foxes twitched their whiskers gratefully

and Sizzle Spiders clapped their front legs.

Tibben waved to Sunako the Sand Elf, who was standing by a pile of shiny blue Water Crystals.

"Thank you, Potions Apprentice," called Sunako, waving back.

Tibben looked down and saw a trail of Oil Ants happily walking by. They waggled their antennae in salute.

Soon they were at the edge of the desert; they could see Troll Bridge to the east. Cragg the Quarry Troll stood waiting to see them as they passed. A small troll was sitting on his shoulders and waving frantically. "Thank you, Tibben. Thank you, Wizz," said the troll as they walked by. "My garden's much better now!"

"Thank you!" squeaked the little troll, and as Tibben and Wizz entered Steadysong Forest, they heard him say in an excited voice, "Daddy! Was that really the next Potions Master?"

Tibben looked at Wizz nervously. He had suddenly realized: now that he had five **Glints** he could take the Master's Challenge to become a Potions Master, just like Grandpa.

"Oh, Wizz," he said, "I hope I can pass it!"

"No worry wooz," she said, and took his hand in her paw. "Wizz and Tibben together."

"Yes," said Tibben. "We'll do it together."

Hand in paw, they ran through Steadysong Forest, all the way to the largest tree in the kingdom, where Grandpa was waiting for them.

"Grandpa! Grandpa!" cried Tibben. "I got my fifth **Glint**! I got **Diamond**!"

Grandpa beamed. "Well done, Tibben," he said. "I always knew you could do it." He patted his pocket. "The *Master's Dial* is pointing to Harmony again."

He gave Tibben a huge hug.

"We met the Firebird!" Tibben told him with pride. "And Wizz found Fire Lily!"

"Little Wizz! That's amazing!" said Grandpa. "Fire Lily is a very rare plant indeed. Usually only the Firebird can find it."

"Tib Tib help," said Wizz.

"I made Second Sight Potion," Tibben said.

"That was clever, Tibben. Good thinking!" Grandpa opened his arms to join Wizz in the group hug. "I'm so proud of my special team," he said. "You and Wizz are so strong together. You helped the Firebird and brought back Harmony, and now we have a whole new challenge ahead."

"The Master's Challenge?" said Tibben.

"Yes," said Grandpa.

"Wizz help?" Wizz asked.

"Yes, Wizz. You can help Tibben." He hugged them both tightly. "I know that together you can do it."

The three friends sat with their arms around each other until the

sun set on the forest and it was time
to go into the Potions Shop and
have a cup of Hazelwood tea.

Potions

Extracts from *The Book of Potions*:

Blooming Brew

Effect: Makes anything healthy
Ingredients:
- Vary Violet
- Mouse Water
- Glow Root

Budding Potion

Effect: Makes plants flower
Ingredients:
- Grass Berries
- Stretch Thistle

Cooling Potion

Effect: Cools the drinker for one hour
Ingredients:
- Ice Fern
- Dark Water
- Chilly Seeds

Dreaming Potion

Effect: Gives drinker a lovely long dream
Ingredients:
- Cloud Lotus
- Sleeping Willow

Firework Liquid

Effect: Creates a spectacular firework display
Ingredients:
- Spark Leaf
- Flame Thorn

Hover Potion

Effect: Causes drinker to hover for two hours
Ingredients:
- Golden Root
- Cloud Lotus
- Light Puff

Iron Cream
Effect: Repairs and toughens shell, horn and bone
Ingredients:
- Strong Scale
- Pearly Shell
- Dwarfsteel

Long Beard Gel
Effect: Gives drinker a super long beard
Ingredients:
- Unicorn Whisker
- Stretch Thistle

Second Sight Potion
Effect: Lets a Gatherer find rare items for 30 minutes
Ingredients:
- Water Crystal
- Antenna Hairs
- Glass Berries

Sharpening Ointment
Effect: Sharpens horns, teeth, knives and swords
Ingredients:
- Pepper Nettle
- Diamond Powder

Shrinking Potion
Effect: Makes the drinker shrink in size for ten minutes
Ingredients:
- Vary Violet
- Mouse Water
- Low Root

Singsong Potion
Effect: Keeps birds and mermaids in tune
Ingredients:
- Steady Leaf
- Tuning Shell

Tail Powder
Effect: Gives drinker an impressive tail
Ingredients:
- Long Cane
- Stretch Thistle
- Brine Serpent Skin

Trail Powder
Effect: Increases tracking skill for one day
Ingredients:
- Snout Grass
- Scent of the Valley
- Quick Sand

Ingredients

Extracts from
The Glossary of Magic Ingredients

Antenna Hairs
Given in gratitude by the Oil Ants of the Parched Desert. Used in **Second Sight Potion**

Brine Serpent Skin
Given in gratitude by serpents of the Fickle Ocean. Used in **Tail Powder**

Chilly Seeds
Found in the Frozen Tundra. Used for **Cooling Potion**

Cloud Lotus
Floats on Lake Sapphire. White fluffy plant. Key ingredient in Flying and Floating Potions as well as **Dreaming Potion, Hover Potion, Rooting Potion, Waterskate Powder** and **Rain Potion**

Dark Water
Found in caves. Used for **Rain Potion** and **Cooling Potion**

Diamond Powder
Made from grinding diamonds from the Diamond Mines. Used for **Glitter Dust, Sharpening Ointment** and **Shine Potion**

Dwarfsteel
Exchange with Ice Dwarfs in the Frozen Tundra. Used for **Magic Rope** and **Iron Cream**

Fire Lily

Extremely rare ingredient. Used to make Firebird nests

Flame Thorn

Found in the Parched Desert. Used for **Firework Liquid**

Glass Berries

Round, see-through berries found under sand in the Parched
Desert. Used in **Second Sight Potion**

Glow Root

Found in the Tangled Glade. Used for **Health Potions**

Golden Root

Grows underground in Moonlight Meadow. Look for golden
flower and dig under left side. Used for **Flying Potion,
Floating Potion, Hover Potion** and **Rooting Potion**. Store
underground

Grass Berries

Green berries found on Troll Plains. Used in **Budding Potion**

Ice Fern

Found in the Frozen Tundra. Used for **Cooling Potion**

Long Cane

Found in Troll Hills. Used for **Tail Powder**

Low Root

Found in Moonlight Meadow.
Used for **Shrinking Potion**

Mouse Water
Collect from Mouse Pond. Used for **Shrinking Potion** and
Blooming Brew

Pearly Shell
Found inside salt-water clamshells deep in the Fickle Ocean.
Used for **Iron Cream**

Pepper Nettle
Found in the Parched Desert. Used for **Sharpening Ointment**

Red-Hot Orchid
Found in Steadysong Forest. Used for **Exploding Powder**

Scent of the Valley
Found in Steadysong Forest. Used in **Trail Powder**

Shelter Leaf
Picked at the southern edge of **Steadysong Forest**

Sleeping Willow
Found in Lake Sapphire. Pick at midnight. Used in
Dreaming Potion

Snout Grass
Found in Green Silk Grasses. Used for **Trail Powder**

Spark Leaf
Found in the Parched Desert. Used for **Firework Liquid**

Steady Leaf
Found in Steadysong Forest. Used for **Balance Potion,
Waterskate Powder** and **Singsong Potion**

Stretch Thistle

Grows in the Green Silk Grasses. Tall, green, spiky plant. Used for **Growth Potions, High Reach Potion, Arm Stretch Cream** and **Ten Legs Potion**

Strong Scale

Exchange with fish in the Fickle Ocean for **Swim Fast Gel**. Used for **Iron Cream**

Tuning Shell

Found at the bottom of the Fickle Ocean. Used in **Singsong Potion**

Unicorn Whisker

Exchange with Twilight Unicorns on Moonlight Meadow for **Diamond Powder.** Used in all **Speed Potions, Hair Potions** and **Regeneration Potions**

Vary Violet

Found in Frozen Tundra. Used for **Change Potions**

Water Crystal

Found under the sand in the Parched Desert. Provides clean fresh water for desert creatures. Also used in **Second Sight Potion**

Tibben's Quiz

1. At what age is Grandpa planning to retire to the Vale of Years?

2. Where does the Twilight Unicorn live?

3. Instead of **Trail Powder**, which potion does Tibben accidentally make for a Hunting Imp?

4. Which powder contains **Red-Hot Orchid**?

5. Which words are missing from the following two sentences?

Soon they came to the southern edge of Steadysong _____.

Now they had to cross the _____ Plains to reach the Parched _____.

6. Where do elves usually live?

7. Which three things does Seraphin bring to the kingdom?

8. At the end of Tibben and Wizz's journey, which drink do Grandpa, Tibben and Wizz enjoy together?

Turn to the back of the book for answers to this quiz!

Missing Glints

The names of these **Glints** are missing
some letters! Can you help Tibben by
filling in the blanks?

1. _R_STA_

2. O_A_

3. PE_ _ L

4. _UB_

5. DI_ _ ON_

Turn to the back of the book for answers to this quiz!

Follow the Trail

Tibben is frantically trying to find *Glass Berries* to make Second Sight Potion, but there are so many different ingredients that he keeps mixing them up!

Can you help him follow the trail to find the key final ingredient?

Turn to the back of the book for answers to this quiz!

Solutions

Quiz Answers

1. 100 years of age
2. Moonlight Meadow
3. Tail Powder
4. Exploding Powder
5. Forest; Troll; Desert
6. Blue Mountain
7. Warmth; Energy; Life
8. Hazelwood tea

Missing Glints Solution

Crystal • Opal • Pearl • Ruby • Diamond

Follow the Trail